For Dave and Nuno

First published 2015
Published by Butterfly Books Limited

All enquiries to info@butterflybooks.uk

ISBN: 978-0-9932769-2-7

A CIP catalogue record for this book is available from the British Library.

Printed in England.

Edited by Corey Brotherson

A special thank you to The WaterSafe Installers' Scheme, Carol Cannavan and
The Chartered Insitute of Plumbing and Heating Engineering (CIPHE).

My Mummy is a
PLUMBER

By Kerrine Bryan & Jason Bryan

Illustrated by Marissa Peguinho

My mummy is a plumber,
her job sounds really grand.
She likes to wear blue overalls,
with a toolbox in her hand.

She starts off in her office,
preparing for her day.

Designing pipework on her computer,
and then she's on her way!

Mr Brown from Pickleton Town,
had a problem one winter's morning.
The pipes in his loft had frozen,
and burst without any warning!

Drip, drop, drip, drop...
Whoops! Whoosh! Yelp!
Water, water everywhere,
but mummy is here to help!

Mummy searches her toolbox...
A silver spanner, hooray!

Klink, klank, klink, klank,
mummy saves the day!

Mrs Platt from the upstairs flat,
bought a picture with spots and stripes,

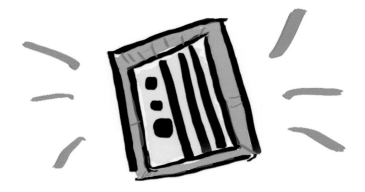

but when she tried to put it up,
the nail went through a pipe!

Splish, splosh, splish, splosh...
Whoops! Whoosh! Yelp!

Water, water everywhere,
but mummy is here to help!

Mummy searches her toolbox...
Pipe cutters, hooray!

Snip, snap, snip, snap, mummy saves the day!

Now Suzy Pane from Chudberry Lane,
her toilet was so blocked,
that every time she flushed it,
the water never stopped.

Slush, gush, slush, gush...
Whoops! Whoosh! Yelp!

Water, water everywhere,
but mummy is here to help!

Mummy searches her toolbox...
A red plunger, hooray!

Splidge, splodge, splidge, splodge,
mummy saves the day!

Drip, drop, splish, splosh,
slush, gush, yelp!

I might try some plumbing too,
and like mummy be ready to help!

Snip, snap, klink, klank,
splidge, splodge, hooray!
Maybe in the future,
I can save the day!